CHARLIE
Goes to School

For all the dedicated, devoted, hardworking teachers
in the world. Thank you.
—Ree

ISBN 978-0-06-221920-6

The artist used Winsor & Newton watercolor paint over digital art on
140 lb. Arches hot-press paper to create the illustrations for this book.
Typography by Rachel Zegar
13 14 15 16   LP   10 9 8 7 6 5 4 3 2
❖
First Edition

When cooking, it is important to keep safety in mind. Children should always ask permission from an adult before
cooking and should be supervised by an adult in the kitchen at all times. The publisher and author disclaim any liability
from any injury that might result from the use, proper or improper, of the recipe contained in this book.

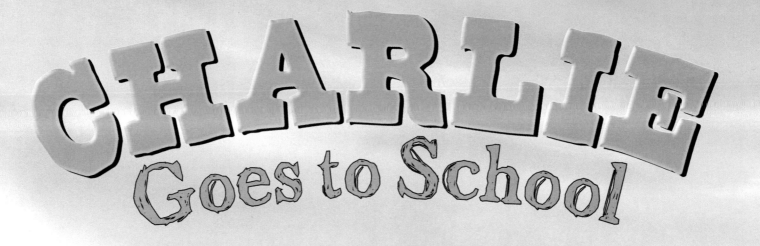

CHARLIE
Goes to School

by Ree Drummond

illustrations by Diane deGroat

HARPER

An Imprint of HarperCollinsPublishers

Oh, hello!

Charlie the Ranch Dog here.
Things are sure busy around
the ol' homestead today!

Daddy's busy fixing a tire.

I'm helping, of course.

Cowboy Josh is busy shoeing a horse.

He'd never be able to do it without me.

The cows are busy taking care of their calves. . . .

Okay, so I can't help out much there.

As for Mama, she's busy in the house with the kids.
I'd better get in there and lend a hand! I imagine
Mama could use a little help right about now.
I'm Charlie the Ranch Dog, after all.
This place would simply fall apart if I wasn't here.

What's everybody doing?
I see books. . . .
I see a chalkboard. . . .
Hmm . . .

Why, I do believe . . .
Why, I do believe they're doing

SCHOOL!

I remember school! Mama told me all about it. Lots of kids go to school at *school*, and lots of kids go to school at *home*.

My family goes to school at home.
It's lots and lots of fun.
There's math time . . .

I love math. Especially the subtraction part.

And there's reading time . . .
Those are definitely the strangest-looking cows
I've ever seen!

There's also recess time!
It's important for the kids to
get lots of exercise.

I should know. Exercise is a
way of life for me.

And best of all, there's snack time.

YUM.

Snack time is my life.

After snack time, it's time to get back inside
and hit the books!

Hey . . . I have an idea.

Suzie needs to learn her letters. They come in handy when it comes to reading about food. Here, for instance, the letters say, "This food is only for Charlie. Please do not touch."

"FOCUS, SUZIE. FOCUS!"

Kitty Kitty needs to practice his math.
Numbers are very important when it comes
to counting food.

"DON'T PLAY, KITTY KITTY. COUNT!"

The ranch horses need to brush up on
their history.

"EXCUSE ME! BOOKS AREN'T FOR EATING!"

And Walter? Well, Walter needs to learn everything!

ZZZZZZZ

"SLEEPING? HOW CAN YOU SLEEP AT A TIME LIKE THIS?"

Wait a minute . . .
What in the world is going on around here?

"**CLASS!** If you don't start working on your school, there will definitely be no snack today. Now help me get this place cleaned up before Mama sees it!"

Whew! This school business sure is hard work! I think I need a recess.

Yawn

Or maybe . . . YAWN . . . maybe a nap would be better.

I can always start my school again tomorrow.

Charlie's Favorite Strawberry Oatmeal Bars

Makes 24 bars

Be safe! Always cook with an adult. Don't touch sharp knives or hot stoves and ovens! And always wash your hands before and after cooking.

Ingredients

1¾ sticks salted butter, cut into pieces, plus
   more for greasing pan
1½ cups all-purpose flour
1½ cups rolled oats
1 cup packed brown sugar
1 teaspoon baking powder
½ teaspoon salt
1 (10- to 12-ounce) jar strawberry preserves

Instructions

1. Preheat the oven to 350 degrees. Butter a 9x13-inch rectangular pan.

2. Mix together the butter, flour, oats, brown sugar, baking powder, and salt.

3. Press half the oat mixture into the prepared pan. Spread a thin layer of the strawberry preserves on top.

4. Sprinkle the other half of the oat mixture over the preserves and pat lightly so as not to disturb the bottom layers.

5. Bake until light brown, 30 to 40 minutes. Let cool completely, then cut into squares! Serve with a glass of cold milk.

Note: You can use any kind of jam or preserves you like! (Apricot is delicious.)